From Pixels To Page

Mrigendra Bharti

Published by Sellbrochure Vymish Entertainment, 2024.

This is a work of fiction. Similarities to real people, places, or events are entirely coincidental.

FROM PIXELS TO PAGE

First edition. June 21, 2024.

Copyright © 2024 Mrigendra Bharti.

ISBN: 979-8227874245

Written by Mrigendra Bharti.

Table of Contents

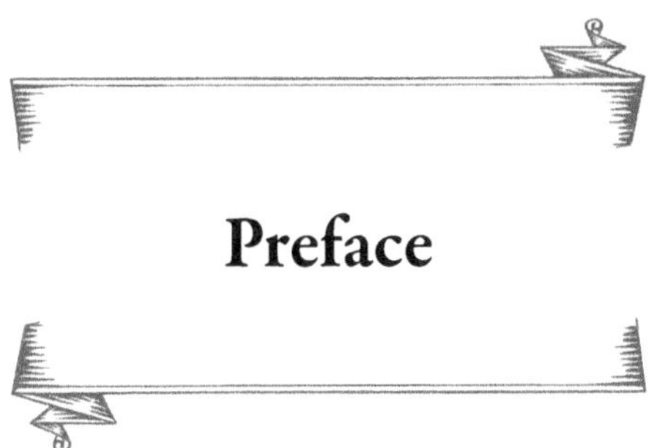

Preface

This book holds within its pages a story born not in the solitude of a writer's garret, but in the vibrant hum of an online forum. It's a tale of friendship forged over shared dreams and fueled by the boundless potential of the written word.

Ethan, an introvert yearning for connection, and Olivia, a writer grappling with self-doubt, found solace and inspiration in each other's words. Their initial online interactions, hesitant and tentative, blossomed into a collaboration that defied expectations.

Within these chapters, you'll witness the birth of "The Quirky Quills," a series that captured the hilarious struggles and triumphs of aspiring writers. You'll journey with Ethan and Olivia as they navigate the dizzying world of literary success, their friendship a constant anchor amidst the whirlwind of fame.

But this story delves deeper than awards ceremonies and bestseller lists. It explores the transformative power of collaboration, the way shared passion can ignite creativity and push boundaries. It celebrates the unexpected beauty of friendship, a bond forged in the digital realm and nurtured in the warmth of shared experiences.

As you turn the pages, prepare to be transported on a journey of laughter, growth, and self-discovery. This is a story about the power of words, the magic of connection, and the enduring echoes of inspiration that resonate long after the virtual world fades to black.

Let the story begin...

Prologue

The whirring of a dial-up modem cut through the silence, a symphony of beeps and squawks heralding a connection forged not of wires and circuits, but of shared dreams and hidden desires. In the pre-dawn hush, Ethan squinted at the flickering glow of his computer monitor, his fingertips hovering over the keyboard. Tonight, like countless nights before, he ventured into the online forum, a haven for aspiring writers, seeking not just critique but a kindred spirit.

Across the city, bathed in the soft light of a bedside lamp, Olivia typed furiously, her brow furrowed in concentration. The frustration of a writer's block gnawed at her, her confidence dwindling with each deleted sentence. With a sigh, she logged onto the forum, a desperate hope flickering within her.

In the vast, digital landscape of the forum, their paths collided for the first time. A thread titled "Quirky Characters in Crisis" sparked their initial interaction, hesitant words transforming into lively discussions. They dissected plot twists, dissected grammar, and offered solace in the face of creative roadblocks.

Ethan, initially shy, found himself drawn to Olivia's sharp wit and insightful observations. Olivia, in turn, discovered a wellspring of empathy and unyielding encouragement in Ethan's thoughtful replies. Under the cloak of anonymity, their true selves began to emerge, a vulnerability born from the shared yearning to translate dreams into words.

Little did they know, this fleeting spark ignited in the digital world would blossom into a collaboration that would change their lives, a testament to the extraordinary connections that can bloom even amidst the anonymity of the online world. As Ethan typed his final message for the night, a question hung in the air — a question that would set their story in motion: "Would you ever consider collaborating on a project?"

And so, amidst the whirring of modems and the flickering glow of computer screens, a friendship bloomed and a journey began. In the chapters that follow, you'll witness the transformation of those online interactions, the birth of a story fueled by shared passion, and the enduring power of words that transcended the boundaries of the digital realm.

Acknowledgement

This book wouldn't exist without the countless cups of coffee (and tea!) that fueled late-night writing sessions. It wouldn't exist without the quiet corners of coffee shops and the comforting solitude of home offices that provided the space for imagination to take flight.

Gratitude extends to the vibrant online communities and cherished forums that fostered a love of storytelling and offered a platform for early ideas to take root. A special thanks goes out to the patient beta readers who provided invaluable feedback and helped shape this story.

Most importantly, this book is dedicated to the power of shared dreams, unexpected connections, and the enduring magic of words that bridge the gap between worlds.

About Sellbrochure Vymish Entertainment

Sellbrochure Vymish Entertainment, recognized as India's largest book publishing company, has made significant strides in ensuring its extensive collection of books reaches audiences across the global market. This rapid expansion is a testament to the company's dedication to disseminating knowledge and literature far beyond national borders. Central to its success is its affiliation with InkWhirl Media Networks, a reputable entity in the media and publication industry known for its innovative and strategic approaches. Within this network, InkWhirl Publication LLC operates as a vital division, further enhancing the company's capabilities and reach in the international market.

The visionary behind this enterprise is Mrigendra Bharti, the founder of Sellbrochure Vymish Entertainment. His foresight and passion for the literary world have been instrumental in steering the company towards remarkable growth and recognition. Under his leadership, Sellbrochure Vymish Entertainment has not only expanded its catalog but also established a strong presence in both domestic and international markets. Mrigendra Bharti's commitment to excellence and innovation has been a driving force in the company's journey, ensuring that it stays ahead of industry trends and meets the evolving needs of readers worldwide.

Sellbrochure Vymish Entertainment operates under the robust support of its parental organization, Mrigendra Bharti Group InfoTech. This affiliation provides the necessary resources and strategic guidance, enabling the publishing company to undertake ambitious projects and explore new markets. Mrigendra Bharti Group InfoTech's extensive experience in technology and information services has been a valuable asset, allowing Sellbrochure Vymish Entertainment to integrate advanced digital solutions in its operations, thereby enhancing its distribution capabilities and reader engagement.

Through relentless efforts and a commitment to quality, Sellbrochure Vymish Entertainment continues to break barriers and expand the reach of Indian literature globally. The company's diverse portfolio includes a wide range of genres, catering to different age groups and interests, thereby fostering a rich and inclusive reading culture. As it continues to innovate and grow, Sellbrochure Vymish Entertainment remains dedicated to its mission of making literature accessible to all, contributing significantly to the global literary landscape.

Connect With Mrigendra,
Thank you very much for choosing this book.
You can also connect with me on Instagram,
https://www.instagram.com/i_mrigendrabharti.official
With Love,
Mrigendra Bharti

Introduction

The hum of the dial-up modem filled the room, a symphony of beeps and squawks heralding Ethan's nightly pilgrimage. He wasn't venturing into a cathedral or a mosque; his sanctuary was the flickering glow of his computer monitor, the gateway to a vibrant online forum for aspiring writers. Here, beneath usernames and avatars, anxieties about self-promotion dissolved, replaced by the raw vulnerability of shared dreams and creative struggles.

Ethan, by nature an introvert, found solace in the anonymity. He could dissect plot twists and grammar mistakes with abandon, offering and receiving critiques without the sting of judgment. Tonight, however, a restlessness gnawed at him. He craved more than just dissecting someone else's work; he yearned for a connection, a kindred spirit who understood the anxieties that plagued him – the fear of rejection, the gnawing self-doubt that whispered he wasn't good enough.

Across the city, bathed in the soft glow of a bedside lamp, Olivia typed furiously. Frustration gnawed at her. The blinking cursor mocked her, a stark reminder of the writer's block that had shackled her creativity for days. She longed for a fresh perspective, a nudge in the right direction. With a sigh, she logged onto the forum, a desperate hope flickering within her.

In the vast, digital landscape, their paths collided for the first time. A thread titled "Quirky Characters in Crisis" sparked their initial interaction. Ethan, under the username "The Inkwell Alchemist," offered a witty observation about a protagonist with a penchant for talking vegetables. Olivia, known as "The Word Weaver," countered with a hilarious anecdote about a hero allergic to adventure. Hesitant words transformed into lively discussions. They dissected plot holes, celebrated clever dialogue, and commiserated over the universal struggles of writer's block.

Ethan found himself drawn to Olivia's sharp wit and insightful observations. Her words crackled with energy, each comment a spark that ignited his own imagination. Olivia, in turn, discovered a wellspring of empathy and unyielding encouragement in Ethan's thoughtful replies. Under the cloak of anonymity, their true selves began to emerge – a vulnerability born from the shared yearning to translate dreams into words.

Days turned into weeks, their online interactions growing more frequent and animated. They delved deeper, discussing their literary influences and confessing their secret ambitions. Ethan secretly dreamed of one day publishing a fantasy novel filled with mythical creatures and epic battles. Olivia, on the other hand, harbored a yearning to write historical fiction, weaving tales of forgotten heroes and bygone eras.

One evening, amidst a particularly heated debate about the ending of a popular fantasy series, Ethan posed a question that hung heavy in the virtual air: "Would you ever consider collaborating on a project?"

The question, seemingly casual, sent a jolt through Olivia. Collaboration? The idea was both daunting and exhilarating.

Could they, two strangers connected by pixels and prose, truly create something together?

Olivia's initial apprehension quickly melted away, replaced by a sense of shared excitement. The concept of collaborating, of weaving their individual strengths and styles into a single narrative, held an undeniable allure. They began brainstorming ideas, bouncing quirky concepts and outrageous plotlines off each other. Ethan's love for fantastical elements meshed with Olivia's historical leanings in unexpected ways.

One particularly inspired night, the idea for "The Quirky Quills" was born. It would be a series chronicling the adventures (and misadventures) of a group of aspiring writers at a fictional writing retreat nestled in the heart of the English countryside. Each character, a caricature of a stereotypical writer's persona, would navigate the challenges and triumphs of the writing life, from battling writer's block to facing their inner critic (hilariously personified as a grumpy, tea-obsessed bulldog named Winston).

Olivia, with her penchant for historical detail, would breathe life into the setting, crafting a whimsical portrayal of the old manor house that served as the retreat center. Ethan, with his flair for the fantastical, would weave humor and unexpected events into the narrative, transforming the writing retreat into a crucible for creativity and outlandish escapades.

The collaborative process flowed with surprising ease. They exchanged chapters via email, each new installment igniting a spark of excitement. Ethan laughed out loud as he read Olivia's description of the retreat's eccentric owner, a flamboyant thespian with a penchant for quoting Shakespeare at every opportunity. Olivia, in turn, was captivated by Ethan's creation of a mischievous spirit named "The Muse," a mischievous entity that bestowed fleeting moments of inspiration on unsuspecting writers (often with hilarious consequences).

As they delved deeper into the world they were creating, a sense of accomplishment

Chapter 1: The Quiet Boy and the Social Butterfly

In the heart of the bustling town of Evergreen, amidst the vibrant hum of everyday life, lived a young boy named Ethan. Unlike his peers who reveled in the social whirl, Ethan found solace in the quiet company of books. His world was one of words and imagination, where he could escape the complexities of real life and immerse himself in fantastical tales of adventure and romance.

Ethan's sanctuary was the town's quaint library, a treasure trove of stories waiting to be discovered. He would spend hours wandering through the aisles, his fingers tracing the spines of countless books, their titles whispering promises of far-off lands and extraordinary characters. Each book was a portal to a new world, a chance to step into someone else's shoes and experience life through their eyes.

Ethan's love for reading was nurtured by his grandmother, a kind-hearted woman who instilled in him a deep appreciation for the written word. She would often regale him with tales of her own childhood, her voice weaving magic as she described far-off places and the people she had met along the way. These stories fueled Ethan's imagination, sparking his curiosity and his desire to explore the world beyond his small town.

As Ethan grew older, his love for books deepened. He devoured novels of all genres, from classic literature to contemporary fiction, from historical epics to science fiction sagas. Each book he read left an indelible mark on his mind, shaping his worldview and expanding his understanding of the human experience.

Ethan's quiet demeanor and love for solitude often set him apart from his peers. He was content to spend his time lost in the pages of a book, his imagination soaring to far-off lands while his classmates engaged in the social whirl of school life. While he enjoyed the company of his friends, he found true fulfillment in the company of his books, his silent companions who never judged him or failed to understand him.

One day, while browsing the library's new arrivals section, Ethan stumbled upon a book that would change his life forever. It was a collection of short stories by an unknown author, and its title, "Whispers from the Heart," immediately caught his attention. Intrigued, he picked up the book and settled into a cozy armchair, eager to delve into its pages.

As Ethan read the stories, he was captivated by the author's vivid descriptions and the depth of the characters' emotions. Each story was a window into a different soul, revealing the joys, sorrows, and dreams of ordinary people. Ethan found himself deeply moved by the stories, his own heart echoing the emotions of the characters.

When he finished the book, Ethan felt a profound sense of connection to the author, as if they had shared a secret language through the written word. He longed to know more about this mysterious writer, to understand the mind that had created such captivating stories.

With a newfound determination, Ethan set out to find the author. He scoured the internet, searched local bookstores, and even inquired with the library staff, but his efforts were in vain. There was no trace of the author, no name or biography to give him a clue about their identity.

Despite the lack of information, Ethan refused to give up. He felt a deep connection to the author's work, and he was determined to find them. He knew that somewhere out there, a kindred spirit was waiting to be discovered, someone who shared his love for words and the power of storytelling.

Ethan's world, for all its richness of imagination, existed primarily within the confines of books and his own mind. The bustling life of Evergreen, with its social gatherings and noisy crowds, felt like a distant echo compared to the fantastical adventures and introspective journeys he embarked on through literature. But one chance encounter on social media was about to disrupt the tranquility of his quiet world.

One evening, while browsing through Instagram, Ethan's thumb paused on a particular profile picture. It belonged to a girl named Olivia, and her smile radiated a warmth that instantly drew Ethan in. Unlike the curated feeds he usually scrolled through, Olivia's page was a vibrant tapestry of her life. Pictures showcased her adventurous spirit - scaling a rock wall, kayaking down a river, exploring a bustling city square. Short videos captured her infectious laughter as she sang along to music or danced in the rain. Every post overflowed with a zest for life that was both captivating and unfamiliar to Ethan.

Intrigued, Ethan ventured deeper into Olivia's profile. Her captions were like mini-stories, weaving narratives around seemingly mundane moments. A picture of a steaming cup of coffee morphed into a humorous anecdote about a late-night study session. A photo of a sunset transformed into a poetic reflection on the beauty of fleeting moments. Ethan found himself drawn not just to Olivia's vivacity but also to the depth hidden beneath the surface.

Hesitantly, Ethan typed out a message. It was a simple "Hi," laced with a nervousness he hadn't felt in years. He wasn't sure what he expected, perhaps just a polite reply or even silence. But to his surprise, Olivia responded almost instantly. Her message was warm and friendly, and soon they were engaged in a conversation that flowed effortlessly.

Ethan discovered that Olivia, despite her outward exuberance, shared a similar love for books. She mentioned her favorite authors, and to his delight, a few of them were his own. They delved into discussions about their favorite characters, debated plot twists, and shared recommendations for hidden gems they had stumbled upon. As they conversed, Ethan felt a sense of connection he hadn't experienced before. Here was someone who understood his passion for the written word, someone who could navigate the fantastical worlds he cherished.

However, unlike Ethan, Olivia thrived on social interaction. Her posts were peppered with mentions of upcoming events with friends, weekend getaways, and impromptu adventures. As Ethan read about these experiences, a pang of envy flickered within him. He yearned to step outside his comfort zone and experience life with the same enthusiasm Olivia displayed. Yet, the thought of navigating social gatherings and small talk filled him with a familiar dread.

Despite their contrasting personalities, Ethan and Olivia found a common ground in their shared love for stories. Their online conversations became a bridge between their vastly different worlds, and Ethan found himself eagerly anticipating their next interaction. A spark of curiosity had ignited within him, a desire to not just read about life's adventures but to experience them firsthand, perhaps with Olivia by his side.

Ethan, his heart pounding with a nervous excitement he hadn't felt before, awaited Olivia's next message. The world of books, his usual sanctuary, seemed to fade away as he became engrossed in their online connection. Gone were the days of solitary evenings spent solely with fictional characters. Now, Olivia's infectious energy and genuine curiosity about his life filled the void.

Their conversations, initially focused on their shared love for literature, blossomed into a vibrant exchange of thoughts and experiences. Ethan, usually reserved and hesitant to share his inner world, found himself opening up to Olivia with a surprising ease. He confided his dreams of one day writing his own story, a secret ambition he had harbored for years. To his surprise, Olivia wasn't just receptive; she was encouraging. Her enthusiastic belief in his talent fueled a spark of confidence within Ethan, a flicker of hope that his dream might not be so far-fetched after all.

As the days turned into weeks, their conversations evolved beyond the written word. They discovered a mutual love for music, sharing playlists filled with songs that resonated with their souls. Late-night video calls became a regular occurrence, their faces glowing in the warm light of their respective screens as they talked for hours, their laughter echoing through the virtual space. Ethan, who once found social interaction draining, discovered a joy in connecting with Olivia that transcended the physical distance that separated them.

Through Olivia's eyes, Ethan began to see the world in a new light. Her stories of spontaneous adventures and her passion for trying new things ignited a curiosity within him. He found himself drawn to her zest for life, a stark contrast to his own comfort in routine and solitude. Olivia, in turn, was intrigued by Ethan's depth of knowledge and his quiet wisdom. She appreciated his ability to listen intently and offer insightful perspectives on the world around them.

Their virtual connection fostered a unique bond. They shared secrets, fears, and aspirations, their vulnerability creating a space of trust and understanding. Ethan, who had always felt like an outsider looking in, finally felt like he belonged. Olivia, with her vibrant personality, had unknowingly become a bridge, connecting him to a world he once thought was out of reach.

Despite the blossoming friendship, a tiny seed of doubt lingered in Ethan's mind. The world of social media, with its carefully curated feeds and filtered photos, presented a one-dimensional version of Olivia's life. He yearned to experience her vivacity firsthand, to see the sparkle in her eyes and the genuine smile that lit up her profile pictures. Yet, the thought of meeting her in person, of navigating the complexities of real-life interaction, filled him with a familiar apprehension. But as their virtual connection deepened, a part of Ethan knew that this online friendship might be on the cusp of something more, something that demanded a leap of faith from his comfort zone.

The line between their online world and Ethan's reality began to blur as their friendship blossomed. Discussions about their favorite books morphed into recommendations for movies they could watch together virtually. Shared playlists evolved into late-night video calls where they sang along, their voices blending in a newfound harmony. Evenings that were once spent lost in the pages of a book were now filled with laughter and animated conversations with Olivia.

Ethan, usually hesitant to share his introverted nature, found himself surprisingly comfortable confiding in Olivia. He spoke about his anxieties around social gatherings and his preference for the quiet solace of books. To his delight, Olivia didn't judge. Instead, she offered a listening ear and shared her own experiences with overcoming social awkwardness. Their vulnerabilities became a bridge, fostering a deeper understanding and a sense of shared humanity.

As their bond strengthened, Ethan discovered a newfound confidence. Olivia's encouragement sparked a desire within him to step outside his comfort zone. He started venturing beyond the library walls, exploring local bookstores and attending author readings. He even joined an online writing forum, his fingers hesitantly typing out the first lines of his own story, fueled by Olivia's unwavering belief in his talent.

Meanwhile, Olivia, through Ethan's eyes, began to appreciate the beauty of quiet contemplation. She tagged him along on virtual tours of museums, and they spent evenings discussing art and history, their conversations a delightful blend of her infectious enthusiasm and his thoughtful insights. Ethan's introspective nature, which he once considered a weakness, became a source of strength in their friendship.

Their virtual connection, though vibrant, couldn't fully contain the burgeoning affection Ethan felt for Olivia. He found himself mesmerized by her laugh, captivated by her intelligence, and drawn to her adventurous spirit. The desire to see her beyond the screen, to experience her vivacity in person, grew stronger with each passing day.

One evening, during a video call, Olivia, sensing a shift in Ethan's demeanor, playfully nudged him. "Ever thought of stepping out of your book world and experiencing life with me sometime?" she asked, a hint of challenge in her voice. Ethan's heart skipped a beat. The question hung in the air, a bridge between their virtual haven and the uncharted territory of real-life encounters. A new chapter, filled with both excitement and trepidation, was about to unfold in their story.

Chapter 2: Blossoming Feelings

Ethan stared at the screen, Olivia's playful question echoing in his mind like a melody on repeat. A kaleidoscope of emotions swirled within him, threatening to burst from their confines. Stepping outside his comfort zone had always been a daunting prospect, but the thought of experiencing life with Olivia, of seeing the world through her vibrant eyes, sent a thrill coursing through him. It was like a scene straight out of a coming-of-age novel he'd devoured, a hesitant hero venturing forth on an exhilarating adventure. Yet, a nagging fear lingered, a dark cloud threatening to cast a shadow over his newfound hope. Could their online connection, built on shared interests and a comfortable camaraderie, translate into the complexities of a face-to-face encounter? Would the spark that ignited in the digital realm fizzle out in the harsh light of reality?

Days bled into weeks, and Olivia's question continued to haunt Ethan. He found himself drawn to her profile picture with an intensity that surprised him. Her smile, once a friendly greeting, now held a hidden message, a secret code only his heart seemed to decipher. Her late-night texts, once filled with casual banter about books and movies, now carried a subtle warmth that made his cheeks flush and his heart race a frantic tattoo against his ribs. He began to dissect every word, every laugh, every quirk, searching for any hidden clue that might suggest Olivia reciprocated his feelings. But her messages remained resolutely friendly, devoid of any romantic undertones. Was he reading too much into things? Was his imagination, fueled by his burgeoning affection, painting a picture that didn't exist?

Ethan's internal conflict mirrored the struggle between his introverted nature and the burgeoning emotions for Olivia. The quiet solitude that once brought him solace now felt stifling. The fictional worlds he escaped into no longer held the same allure. The fantastical adventures of his favorite characters paled in comparison to the real-life adventure brewing within him. His mind was consumed by Olivia, by the desire to bridge the gap between their virtual connection and the uncharted territory of his heart. He yearned to see the sparkle in her eyes that her profile picture only hinted at, to hear the infectious laughter that echoed through their video calls in person. But the fear of rejection, of shattering the delicate balance of their friendship, held him back like an invisible anchor, tethering him to the safety of the online world.

Confessing his feelings felt like a gamble, a risky bet with potentially devastating consequences. If Olivia didn't feel the same way, the awkwardness could irreparably damage their friendship, a thought that sent a pang of despair through him. He replayed conversations in his head, searching for any hidden message, any subtle hint that might give him the courage to take the leap. But the more he analyzed their interactions, the more doubt gnawed at him. Perhaps their friendship was built solely on shared interests, a comfortable haven with no room for deeper emotions.

The weight of his unconfessed feelings began to take a toll on Ethan. His usual focus on his studies waned, replaced by a constant preoccupation with Olivia. The books that once transported him to fantastical worlds now lay abandoned, their pages gathering dust. Even the solace of writing, his secret passion, eluded him. The blank page mocked him, his mind unable to conjure the fantastical tales that once flowed effortlessly from his pen. He was adrift in a sea of uncertainty, his emotions a tangled mess, and Olivia, the beacon of hope and excitement, remained just out of reach.

ETHAN'S INTERNAL STRUGGLE intensified with each passing day. The burden of his unspoken feelings became a heavy weight on his chest, a constant reminder of the decision he needed to make. Should he risk jeopardizing their cherished friendship by confessing his love, or should he remain silent and endure the quiet pain of unrequited affection?

He confided in his grandmother, the one person who had always understood the complexities of his introverted nature. Her kind eyes held a lifetime of wisdom as she listened patiently to his tale. In her gentle voice, she spoke of the power of honesty and the importance of taking chances. "Love is a risk, my dear," she said, her hand resting comfortingly on his. "But the greatest regret is often the chance you didn't take."

Her words resonated with Ethan, sparking a flicker of hope within him. Could honesty truly be the answer? Perhaps by confessing his feelings, he could finally move forward, regardless of the outcome. But the fear of rejection remained a formidable obstacle. He envisioned a future devoid of Olivia's laughter, their late-night conversations a faded memory. The thought filled him with a despair so profound it threatened to consume him.

Ethan sought solace in the familiar comfort of books. He delved into novels filled with stories of love and loss, searching for answers within the fictional narratives. He read tales of star-crossed lovers, forbidden romances, and declarations of undying devotion. While some stories offered bittersweet endings, others celebrated the triumph of love, reminding him that even the risk of rejection could be eclipsed by the joy of reciprocation.

His literary exploration provided a sense of perspective, but the question of Olivia's feelings remained a gnawing uncertainty. Did she see him the same way? Did his quiet nature and introverted tendencies hold the same appeal to her as her infectious energy did to him? The lack of any romantic undertones in her messages fuelled his doubts. Perhaps their connection was solely a platonic haven, a friendship built on shared interests that wouldn't survive the transition to a deeper bond.

Ethan's internal conflict manifested in real life. He became withdrawn from his friends and family, his usual quiet demeanor morphing into a brooding silence. The world lost its vibrancy, the bustling town of Evergreen seeming to exist in muted tones. The things that once brought him comfort – reading, writing, even the solace of his solitude – now felt hollow and uninspired. He was suspended in a state of emotional limbo, paralyzed by the weight of his unconfessed love.

One evening, during their usual video call, Olivia, sensing a shift in Ethan's demeanor, inquired about his withdrawn nature.

Her genuine concern, coupled with the warmth in her eyes, ignited a spark of courage within him. He yearned to tell her everything, to unload the burden of his emotions and lay his heart bare. But the words seemed to catch in his throat, choked by fear and uncertainty. The moment stretched on, the silence heavy with unspoken emotions.

Finally, Olivia, her voice laced with concern, spoke. "Ethan, is there something you want to tell me?" The question hung in the air, a challenge and an opportunity rolled into one. Ethan stared at the screen, his heart pounding in his chest. This was the moment of truth. Would he choose to finally open his heart and risk everything, or would he retreat back into the safety of his silence?

Ethan stared back at Olivia on the screen, her face a mixture of concern and curiosity. Her question echoed in his mind, a stark ultimatum that forced him to confront the turmoil within him. The silence stretched, charged with the weight of his unvoiced emotions. The words he longed to say threatened to bubble over, but fear kept them trapped like a dam holding back a torrent.

The thought of losing Olivia, their friendship dissolving like a sandcastle under a crashing wave, filled him with a fresh wave of despair. But the alternative, the suffocating silence that had become his prison, was equally unbearable. He had to know, even if it meant risking the heartbreak of rejection.

Taking a deep breath, Ethan braced himself. His fingers trembled as he typed a message, each word carefully chosen to express the tumultuous emotions churning within him. He poured his heart out, detailing the journey of their friendship, from their initial online connection to the deep bond they had forged. He confessed his admiration for her intelligence, her vibrancy, and the way she had challenged him to step outside his comfort zone.

With a trembling hand, he hit send, his heart pounding a frantic rhythm against his ribs. The wait was agonizing. Every tick of the clock resonated like a drumbeat in the suffocating silence. Finally, a notification popped up – Olivia was typing. He watched with bated breath as her message slowly appeared on the screen.

Her words struck him like a physical blow. Olivia expressed her gratitude for his honesty and the depth of their friendship. But, as Gently as she could, she revealed that she didn't share his romantic feelings. Her heart, she explained, belonged elsewhere.

Ethan reread her message, each word a fresh stab of pain. The world around him seemed to blur, the vibrant colors of Olivia's profile picture leaching away, replaced by a dull grey emptiness. The rejection he had feared for so long had finally materialized, leaving a gaping hole in his chest.

The disappointment was profound, a bitter pill he had to swallow. The friendship they nurtured, the shared laughter, the late-night conversations – did it all mean nothing more to her than just a casual online connection? A tear escaped his eye, tracing a warm path down his cheek. He quickly wiped it away, the sting of humiliation adding to his heartbreak.

The silence on the screen stretched on, heavy with the weight of his unspoken response. What could he say? How could he express the jumble of emotions – the hurt, the confusion, the lingering affection – that swirled within him? Finally, a choked sob escaped his lips. Olivia, sensing his despair, offered words of comfort, assuring him that their friendship still mattered.

Ethan, his voice thick with emotion, managed a weak reply. He needed time, he mumbled, to process his feelings, to navigate this sea of heartbreak. With a heavy heart, he ended the call, the familiar glow of his computer screen now a stark reminder of the connection he had so desperately longed to take to the next level.

Alone in his room, the silence seemed deafening. The weight of rejection pressed down on him, stealing the breath from his lungs. He buried his face in his pillow, the tears finally flowing freely. The future, once filled with the promise of shared experiences with Olivia, now stretched before him like a bleak and uncharted landscape. He had to pick up the pieces of his shattered heart, rebuild his confidence, and find a way to move forward, even if that meant navigating the path of their friendship with Olivia in a new and uncertain light.

The days that followed were shrouded in a heavy fog for Ethan. The initial sting of rejection had given way to a dull ache that lingered in his chest. He moved through his days in a daze, the vibrant colors of the world muted by the pain of his unrequited feelings. Olivia's absence from their usual online routine created a void, a constant reminder of the connection he so deeply missed.

Sleep offered no solace. Ethan's dreams were a chaotic tapestry of shared memories and unspoken words. He'd wake up with a gasp, the remnants of Olivia's laughter echoing in his ears, only to be confronted by the harsh reality of her rejection. He found it difficult to face his friends and family, their well-meaning inquiries about his withdrawn demeanor a constant source of irritation.

He revisited Olivia's message countless times, dissecting every word, searching for any hidden meaning he might have missed. Did she perhaps choose her words carefully to soften the blow? Was there a flicker of hope behind her gentle rejection? His heart desperately clung to these faint possibilities, only to be crushed by the weight of reality.

One afternoon, while aimlessly browsing the library stacks, a book cover caught his eye. It was the same collection of short stories by the unknown author that had initially sparked his online connection with Olivia. Memories flooded back – their late-night discussions dissecting the characters, their shared laughter over humorous anecdotes. A wave of emotions swept over him – a bittersweet cocktail of nostalgia, regret, and a flicker of defiance.

On a whim, Ethan picked up the book and settled into a corner, determined to lose himself in the world of stories. As he read, a sense of calm began to settle over him. The author's evocative prose transported him to different realities, offering a temporary escape from his own heartache. With each story, he found himself appreciating the beauty of language and the power of storytelling.

A spark ignited within him. He remembered his grandmother's words about the importance of taking chances. Perhaps his unrequited love for Olivia wasn't the end of the story, but rather an unexpected turn, a detour that could lead him down a new path. He rummaged through his desk, pulling out a dusty notebook – a repository of his forgotten dreams. With a newfound resolve, he began to write, pouring his emotions and experiences into the blank pages.

The words flowed freely, weaving a tale of a young boy who finds solace in a world of books. The boy's journey mirrored Ethan's own – his introverted nature, his blossoming love for a girl who sees him differently, and ultimately, his discovery of self-expression through the power of writing. As he wrote, a sense of catharsis washed over him. The pain of rejection didn't disappear, but it began to lessen, replaced by a glimmer of hope.

Days turned into weeks, and Ethan's notebook filled with stories. He discovered a hidden passion for writing, a talent that Olivia had encouraged him to explore. The heartbreak of rejection had become a catalyst for his creative fire, fueling his determination to express himself through his own words.

One evening, as he finished writing a particularly poignant scene, Ethan noticed a notification pop up on his computer. It was an email from Olivia. His heart skipped a beat, a surge of anticipation coursing through him. He clicked on the email, prepared for anything.

Olivia's message was brief but heartfelt. She apologized for the delay and wished him well on his writing journey. She mentioned coming across his name on a local literary forum, a platform where aspiring writers shared their work and received feedback. She had read a snippet of his story and was impressed by his talent. Encouraging him to continue writing, she ended the email with a simple "Best, Olivia."

Ethan reread her message a thousand times, a smile slowly spreading across his face. It wasn't the romantic response he had longed for, but it was something more. It was a flicker of hope, a bridge between their past connection and a future filled with possibility. He realized that while his love for Olivia might not be reciprocated, their friendship, built on shared passion and mutual respect, could still exist, albeit in a new form.

With a newfound sense of purpose, Ethan closed his laptop and looked out the window. The world, once shrouded in a gray haze, seemed brighter. He had a story to tell, a voice to share, and a future that stretched before him, filled with the promise of words and the possibility of new beginnings. As he stepped out into the dusk, he knew that while his journey with Olivia had taken an unexpected turn, it was his story to write, and he was finally ready to pen the next chapter.

Chapter 3: The Power of Words

Weeks bled into months, and Ethan's world began to revolve around his newfound passion for writing. The sting of rejection had dulled, replaced by a quiet determination to hone his craft. Every spare moment was dedicated to penning his story, the tale of the introverted boy finding solace in the written word. As he poured his experiences onto the pages, the fictional narrative mirrored his own journey, blurring the lines between reality and imagination.

The online literary forum Olivia had mentioned became a crucial stepping stone in his writing evolution. He posted snippets of his work under a pseudonym, hesitant at first but emboldened by a newfound confidence. The feedback from fellow aspiring writers was encouraging, their praise fueling his desire to improve. He delved into discussions about writing techniques, character development, and the intricacies of plot structure, his thirst for knowledge growing with each passing day.

The forum also brought a sense of community, a group of like-minded individuals who shared his passion for storytelling. He engaged in lively online debates, critiqued other writers' work, and offered his own insights honed by years of devouring countless novels. The camaraderie, albeit virtual, helped him overcome his introverted nature, reminding him that his voice, once confined to the pages of his notebooks, could now resonate with others.

One evening, as Ethan was scrolling through the forum, a new post caught his eye. Titled "A Glimpse into the Butterfly's World," the story revolved around a vivacious young woman yearning for adventure and connection. The author's vivid descriptions and insightful observations resonated with Ethan on a deeper level. As he read further, a sense of familiarity bloomed within him. There was a certain vulnerability in the protagonist's character, a yearning for something beyond the surface-level experiences she chronicled, that felt oddly familiar.

A memory flickered in Ethan's mind – a late-night conversation with Olivia, her voice filled with excitement as she described her dream of traveling the world. Could this be Olivia's story? The pseudonym offered no clues, but the essence of the narrative, the vibrant energy that mirrored Olivia's personality, sent a thrill through him.

The thought of Olivia venturing into the world of writing, of sharing her experiences and innermost thoughts through fictional characters, filled him with a strange mix of emotions. A part of him yearned to know for sure if it was her, to connect with her on a creative level beyond their past friendship. But another part, fueled by a newfound sense of independence, wanted to focus on his own writing journey, free from the expectations of their past connection.

Ethan left a thoughtful comment on the post, praising the author's descriptive language and the depth of the protagonist's character. He signed off with his pseudonym, leaving the door open for a potential conversation without revealing his true identity. The wait for a response stretched long, filled with a nervous anticipation. As the days turned into weeks, doubt began to creep in. Perhaps he had misread the story, projecting his own desires onto the author's words.

Just when Ethan was about to give up hope, a notification popped up – the anonymous author had replied. Their conversation, filled with insightful observations and friendly banter about writing styles and character development, flowed effortlessly. Ethan found himself drawn to the author's witty remarks and insightful analysis, a connection forming based on their shared passion for the written word.

As their online conversations flourished, a flicker of curiosity ignited within Ethan. He yearned to know more about the person behind the pseudonym, the one who seemingly understood his own creative struggles and aspirations. The question of Olivia's identity lingered at the back of his mind, a tantalizing mystery waiting to be unraveled. But as he delved deeper into the world of this anonymous writer, he realized that the answer, at least for now, wasn't the most important thing. He had found a new connection, a fellow traveler on the path of storytelling, and that, in itself, was a story waiting to be written.

THE ONLINE FORUM BECAME a sanctuary for Ethan, a space where he could shed the cloak of his introverted nature and engage in stimulating conversations about writing. His online persona, the one crafted under a carefully chosen pseudonym, allowed him to express himself freely, his voice gaining confidence with each interaction. He discovered a hidden talent for offering constructive criticism, his years of dissecting fictional worlds with Olivia translating into insightful advice for his fellow writers.

The anonymous author behind "A Glimpse into the Butterfly's World" remained a source of fascination for Ethan. Their online exchanges transcended mere critique, evolving into a stimulating dialogue about storytelling. They debated plot twists, dissected character motivations, and shared their own writing anxieties, forging a bond built on mutual respect and a shared passion for the written word.

Ethan couldn't shake the feeling that he knew the author on a deeper level. The way they articulated their thoughts, their witty remarks sprinkled with a hint of vulnerability, mirrored conversations he'd shared with Olivia. But the possibility felt too good to be true. Perhaps he was simply projecting his lingering feelings onto this anonymous writer, clinging to a ghost of the connection they once shared.

One evening, as they were discussing a particularly poignant scene from a new novel, the anonymous author mentioned a specific bookstore Ethan frequented. It was a detail so personal, so specific to their shared history, that a jolt of electricity ran through him. Could it be...? The question hung heavy in the virtual air, a mystery begging to be solved.

The desire to know the truth warred with a newfound appreciation for their anonymous connection. The person behind the pseudonym, whoever they were, had become a confidante, a fellow traveler on the path of storytelling. Their online interactions were a source of inspiration and encouragement, a safe space where Ethan could express his vulnerabilities without fear of judgment.

Torn between his curiosity and the blossoming online friendship, Ethan decided to tread carefully. He crafted a thoughtful message, acknowledging the familiarity in the author's writing and jokingly asking if they frequented a particular bookstore on Elm Street (a subtle nod to their shared history). He hit send, his heart pounding in his chest, a mixture of anticipation and trepidation swirling within him.

The hours that followed stretched on in agonizing silence. Ethan found himself checking the forum every few minutes, his mind replaying every conversation, every detail that might confirm his suspicions. Just as he was about to resign himself to disappointment, a notification popped up on his screen. The anonymous author had replied.

Their response was cryptic, a playful deflection that neither confirmed nor denied his suspicions. They acknowledged the familiarity, attributing it to their shared love for books and the specific genre they were discussing. But they also hinted at a life beyond the online world, a life filled with experiences that mirrored the adventures chronicled in "A Glimpse into the Butterfly's World."

Ethan reread the message several times, a smile playing on his lips. Whether it was Olivia or not, the mystery remained. But one thing was certain – their online connection had taken an unexpected turn. He had found a friend, a fellow storyteller who understood his creative struggles and celebrated his victories. As he logged off for the night, a newfound excitement filled him. The future, once shrouded in uncertainty, now stretched before him, filled with the promise of words, shared dreams, and the possibility of a story yet to be written.

Days turned into weeks, and the online friendship between Ethan and the anonymous author blossomed. Their conversations transcended the realm of writing, venturing into discussions about life, dreams, and aspirations. The author, under the pseudonym "Butterfly Wings," shared tales of travel and adventure, her words painting vivid pictures of exotic landscapes and exhilarating experiences. Ethan, in turn, confided his hopes for his writing career and his growing desire to step outside his comfort zone and engage with the real world beyond the computer screen.

The more they interacted, the stronger Ethan's conviction grew. The playful banter, the insightful observations, the subtle references to their shared past – it all pointed towards one undeniable truth: Butterfly Wings was Olivia. He yearned to confront her, to tear down the veil of anonymity that separated them. But a part of him, hesitant to disrupt the delicate balance of their newfound connection, held him back.

One evening, as they were discussing a particularly poignant scene from a coming-of-age novel, Butterfly Wings mentioned a local author reading she once attended. The details – the date, the venue, the author's name – were an exact match with an event Ethan had attended with Olivia months ago. This confirmation, more definitive than any before, shattered the last vestiges of doubt. It was Olivia, his heart whispered, his online confidante, his fellow storyteller.

The revelation sent a wave of emotions crashing over him. Relief, for finally knowing the truth. Joy, for reconnecting with Olivia, albeit in an unexpected way. But also a flicker of apprehension. How would their online dynamic translate to the complexities of face-to-face interaction? Would the awkwardness of his unrequited feelings cast a shadow on their newfound friendship?

Ethan spent the next few days wrestling with his internal conflict. Finally, he decided to take a chance. In a carefully crafted message, he acknowledged his growing suspicion, playfully hinting at his knowledge of her identity. He expressed his gratitude for their friendship, online and beyond, and offered a simple proposition: wouldn't it be time to meet in person, to bridge the gap between their virtual connection and the reality that had brought them together?

The wait for a response was agonizing. Every notification seemed to hold the potential for Olivia's reply. Finally, after what felt like an eternity, a message popped up. Olivia, under her pseudonym, had responded. Her words were filled with a mixture of surprise and amusement. She admitted to her initial hesitation about revealing her identity but confessed to thoroughly enjoying their online interactions.

She readily agreed to meet, the excitement in her message mirroring Ethan's own. They decided on a neutral location, a cozy coffee shop nestled amidst the bustling town square. As the day of their meeting approached, Ethan felt a nervous flutter in his stomach. He envisioned their encounter, picturing a thousand different scenarios, both hopeful and hesitant.

The day arrived, bathed in the warm glow of the autumn sun. Ethan reached the coffee shop early, his heart pounding a frantic rhythm against his ribs. He scanned the faces in the crowded cafe, searching for a glimpse of Olivia's familiar smile. Just then, a woman walked in, her eyes searching the room. It was her – Olivia, radiating a warmth that transcended the barrier of the computer screen.

Their eyes met, and a smile bloomed on Olivia's face. The awkwardness Ethan feared never materialized. As they settled down and their conversation flowed effortlessly, it felt like a continuation of their online dialogues, albeit with a newfound depth and connection. They reminisced about their online interactions, the shared laughter and vulnerabilities that had fostered their unexpected friendship.

As the afternoon sun began to dip below the horizon, casting long shadows across the cafe tables, they knew it was time to part ways. But there was a lingering sense of a new beginning, a promise of a future friendship built on honesty, mutual respect, and a shared passion for storytelling. With a newfound confidence, Ethan walked Olivia back to her car, the setting sun painting the sky in hues of orange and pink, a reflection of the warmth that bloomed within him.

As they said their goodbyes, a question hung in the air. Was there still a chance for something more, a future where their friendship could blossom into something deeper? The answer remained unwritten, a blank page in their shared story. But for now, Ethan was content with the unexpected turn their relationship had taken. He had found a friend, a confidante, and a fellow traveler on the path of his writing journey. And as he walked back home, the crisp autumn air invigorating him, he knew that this was just the beginning of a new chapter, filled with the promise of words, shared dreams, and a future waiting to be written.

THE COFFEE SHOP ENCOUNTER marked a turning point in Ethan and Olivia's relationship. The initial awkwardness of their unaddressed feelings melted away, replaced by a comfortable camaraderie. They continued their online interactions, their conversations now infused with a newfound layer of understanding and inside jokes born from their shared secret identity.

However, the real magic happened offline. Ethan, emboldened by their in-person meeting, began venturing outside his comfort zone. He joined Olivia on weekend strolls through the park, their discussions ranging from literary analysis to the latest happenings in their lives. He even mustered the courage to participate in a local open mic night, where he nervously read an excerpt from his story to a supportive audience, Olivia cheering him on from the front row.

Their friendship wasn't without its challenges. There were moments when Ethan's old feelings resurfaced, a pang of longing for something more. Olivia, too, grappled with the remnants of her unrequited affection for someone else. But they navigated these moments with honesty and understanding, their shared passion for writing acting as a bridge that kept them connected.

One rainy afternoon, huddled in a cozy bookstore with steaming mugs of hot chocolate, Ethan confided in Olivia about his struggle to capture a pivotal scene in his story. Olivia, ever the perceptive one, pinpointed the root cause – Ethan's fear of putting his vulnerability on the page. She challenged him to embrace his emotions, to channel them into his writing and create a scene that resonated with raw honesty.

Inspired by Olivia's words, Ethan retreated to his room, a newfound determination burning within him. He poured his heart and soul onto the page, laying bare his vulnerabilities and anxieties. As he wrote, a sense of catharsis washed over him. He knew he had finally captured the essence of the scene, the raw emotions mirrored his own journey of self-discovery.

The next day, he shared the revised scene with Olivia, a mix of nervousness and anticipation churning in his stomach. Olivia read it with rapt attention, a tear glistening in her eye as she turned the last page. "Ethan," she said, her voice thick with emotion, "this is beautiful. You've poured your heart into it, and it shows."

Her praise filled him with a sense of accomplishment, a validation that went beyond the written word. It was a testament to the strength of their friendship, a connection built on mutual respect and the courage to be vulnerable.

As the months passed, Ethan's writing flourished. He completed his story, a coming-of-age tale that mirrored his own journey – the introverted boy, the unrequited love, the discovery of confidence through the power of words. He submitted his manuscript to a local literary competition, a flicker of hope burning in his chest.

One evening, as they were browsing the online forum that had brought them together, a notification popped up on Ethan's screen. It was an announcement for the literary competition, revealing the winner. His heart hammered in his chest as he scrolled down the page. There, in bold letters, was his pseudonym, followed by the title of his story.

He turned to Olivia, a wide grin splitting his face. She squealed with delight, her eyes sparkling with excitement. They embraced, a silent celebration of his achievement, a victory not just for him, but for the power of their unique friendship.

As Ethan stood on stage, receiving his award, he scanned the crowd. His eyes met Olivia's, a silent communication passing between them. They had come a long way, their journey taking an unexpected turn, yet leading them to a place of shared joy and personal growth.

Their story, once a tale of unrequited love, had evolved into a beautiful tapestry of friendship, courage, and the transformative power of words. And as Ethan looked towards the future, a future filled with the promise of new stories and endless possibilities, he knew that no matter what path life took them on, their friendship, forged in the online world and nurtured in real life, would forever be a cherished chapter in his heart.

Chapter 4: New Horizons

The bittersweet afterglow of Ethan's literary win lingered in the air. Holding the trophy, a physical manifestation of his months of toil, filled him with a sense of accomplishment. But a more profound realization settled within him – his journey wasn't defined solely by the award. It was the transformative power of writing, the courage to be vulnerable, and the unwavering support of Olivia that truly mattered.

The news of his win spread like wildfire. Friends and family, once bewildered by his introverted nature and newfound passion for writing, showered him with praise. Local newspapers featured his story, and even the online forum buzzed with congratulations from fellow aspiring writers. Ethan, once hesitant to share his voice, was now basking in the unexpected spotlight.

Olivia, his constant cheerleader, became his unofficial publicist. She helped him navigate the newfound attention, suggesting interviews and connecting him with potential mentors within the literary community. Their friendship, once confined to late-night online chats and stolen moments in coffee shops, blossomed into a public partnership, a testament to the unique bond they shared.

Despite the whirlwind of activity, Ethan found time to focus on his writing. The success of his first story fueled his desire to explore new avenues. He delved into various genres, experimenting with his style and voice. Each new piece he wrote reflected not only his evolving perspective but also the influence of the world around him.

One afternoon, while brainstorming ideas for a new story, a conversation with Olivia sparked his imagination. They were discussing the challenges faced by aspiring writers, the constant rejection and self-doubt that plagued even the most successful authors. Suddenly, Ethan envisioned a story – a humorous and poignant tale about a group of quirky writers navigating the treacherous waters of the publishing world.

He excitedly shared his idea with Olivia, her eyes lighting up with enthusiasm. "That's brilliant, Ethan!" she exclaimed. "There's so much potential for humor and relatable characters." She offered to collaborate, to help him flesh out the plot and develop the distinct personalities of the writer protagonists.

Thus began a new chapter in their creative partnership. They spent countless hours discussing character arcs, brainstorming plot twists, and sharing writing samples for feedback. Their online conversations, once focused on dissecting other authors' work, now revolved around their own collaborative creation. The late-night brainstorming sessions, fueled by steaming mugs of coffee and bursts of laughter, were a testament to the joy they found in creating together.

As their collaboration progressed, Ethan realized something profound. His feelings for Olivia, once a source of heartache, had transformed. The initial longing had mellowed into a deep affection and respect, a bond that transcended romantic love.

They were best friends, confidantes, and now, collaborators, their shared passion for writing forming an unbreakable connection.

The future stretched before them, filled with exciting possibilities. Ethan's writing career was blossoming, and their collaborative story held the promise of further success. But beyond the external validation, there was a quiet sense of contentment that resonated within him. He had found his voice, his purpose, and a friend who walked beside him on this extraordinary journey. As he sat down at his computer, ready to tackle the next chapter of their collaborative story, a smile bloomed on his face. He knew, no matter what twists and turns their path held, they would face them together, their words weaving a tapestry filled with laughter, tears, and the unwavering power of friendship.

The collaboration on their new story, aptly titled "The Quirky Quills," proved to be a whirlwind of creativity and laughter. Ethan and Olivia reveled in the process of fleshing out their characters – a world-weary romance novelist battling writer's block, a conspiracy theorist churning out outlandish thrillers, and a flamboyant poet struggling to find an audience. Their contrasting personalities, mirrored in their writing styles, created a hilarious dynamic that spilled over into their real lives.

Their late-night brainstorming sessions evolved into full-blown play readings, as they each adopted the voices of their fictional counterparts, their laughter echoing through Ethan's apartment. As they wrote, they drew inspiration from their own experiences, subtly weaving in anecdotes and inside jokes that only they would understand. The story became a reflection of their unique friendship, a testament to the power of collaboration to transform shared experiences into something hilarious and heartwarming.

Meanwhile, Ethan's literary career continued to gain momentum. Interviews with local publications and online book reviewers catapulted him into the spotlight. He found himself navigating the world of book signings and author talks, the initial awkwardness giving way to a newfound comfort. Olivia, ever the supportive friend, accompanied him to these events, offering moral support and a friendly face in the crowd.

Their public appearances, though initially nerve-wracking for Ethan, turned into unexpected opportunities to connect with readers. Sharing his experiences as a writer, the rejections and triumphs, resonated with aspiring authors. He found himself inspiring others, just as Olivia had once inspired him.

One evening, after a particularly successful book signing, Ethan and Olivia were relaxing at a local cafe. As they sipped their coffee, a woman approached their table, her eyes wide with recognition. "You're Ethan, right?" she asked, her voice filled with excitement. "I loved your story!"

Ethan smiled, surprised by the sudden attention. He spent the next few minutes chatting with the woman, a budding writer who confessed to finding solace and inspiration in his journey. As she walked away, a warmth bloomed within him. He realized that his writing wasn't just about personal expression; it was about connecting with others, offering them a glimpse into his world and hopefully, inspiring them to share theirs.

Looking across the table at Olivia, a sense of gratitude filled him. Their once unexpected friendship had blossomed into something beautiful – a partnership built on trust, shared passion, and a deep respect for each other's dreams. As their eyes met, a silent understanding passed between them. They had embarked on a journey together, a journey of self-discovery and creative exploration. And though the future remained unwritten, they knew they would face it together, their pens poised, ready to continue weaving their stories, side by side.

The success of "The Quirky Quills" surpassed even Ethan and Olivia's wildest dreams. The publishing world embraced the witty narrative, lauding their ability to capture the humorous struggles of aspiring writers. Bookstores buzzed with activity as readers devoured the story, their laughter echoing through the aisles. Ethan and Olivia found themselves catapulted into the national spotlight, their faces gracing magazine covers and their names trending on social media.

Despite the whirlwind of publicity, they remained grounded. They cherished their quiet moments of collaboration, stealing away to Ethan's apartment for brainstorming sessions fueled by coffee and camaraderie. The pressure of success never overshadowed the joy they found in creating together. They knew the heart of their partnership lay in the shared passion, not the external validation.

One evening, as they were finalizing their acceptance speech for a prestigious literary award, a wave of nostalgia washed over Ethan. He looked at Olivia, a silent acknowledgment passing between them. They had come a long way since their first hesitant online interactions. The journey, filled with unexpected turns and emotional detours, had ultimately led them to this moment – a place of shared success and unwavering friendship.

As they stood on the stage, bathed in the spotlight, they delivered their speech. They spoke not just about their individual journeys but about the importance of collaboration, the power of friendship that fueled creativity. They ended their speech with a heartfelt thank you to each other, their voices choked with emotion. The thunderous applause that followed was a testament to the impact their story, both on and off the page, had created.

Life, however, didn't remain a constant whirlwind of award ceremonies and book tours. After the initial frenzy subsided, a sense of normalcy returned. Ethan and Olivia continued writing, exploring new genres and pushing their creative boundaries. They found a comfortable rhythm, balancing their individual writing pursuits with their collaborative projects.

One day, while browsing through a bookstore, Ethan stumbled upon a familiar face on the cover of a new novel. It was Olivia, her name emblazoned above a captivating title. He picked up the book, a surge of pride swelling within him. He knew the story – a heartfelt coming-of-age tale she had hinted at years ago, a story that mirrored her own experiences and dreams.

He spent the following evening engrossed in her novel, transported by her evocative prose and relatable characters. As he finished the last page, a sense of awe settled over him. Olivia, his friend, his confidante, had blossomed into a talented writer in her own right. He realized that their journey wasn't just about their shared success, but about witnessing each other's growth, celebrating each other's triumphs.

Later that week, Olivia surprised Ethan with a manuscript of his own. It was his first attempt at a young adult fantasy novel, a genre he had always been passionate about. He had been hesitant to share it, fearing it wouldn't live up to their collaborative achievements. Olivia, however, saw the potential in his writing, her unwavering belief fueling his confidence.

As they sat together, reading each other's work and offering constructive criticism, a familiar warmth washed over Ethan. They weren't just colleagues or friends; they were each other's biggest supporters, pushing each other to reach their full potential. The future stretched before them, filled with endless possibilities, a shared journey of words and dreams waiting to be written.

And as they turned the final page of their respective stories, a silent promise hung in the air – a promise to keep writing, to keep exploring, to keep supporting each other every step of the way. For theirs wasn't just a story of success, but a story of friendship, a testament to the transformative power of words and the unwavering strength of a bond forged in the unlikeliest of places – the online world – and nurtured in the warmth of real-life connection.

Years flowed by, each chapter filled with the satisfying clatter of keyboards and the quiet hum of creative collaboration. Ethan and Olivia established themselves as literary forces, their individual works garnering critical acclaim and devoted readers. Yet, their partnership remained the cornerstone of their success.

The success of "The Quirky Quills" spawned a series, each book chronicling the hilarious misadventures of their fictional writing ensemble. Readers eagerly awaited each new installment, finding solace and humor in the characters' struggles and triumphs. Ethan and Olivia, reveling in their collaborative success, took turns writing chapters, their distinct styles weaving a seamless tapestry that resonated with a wide audience.

Despite their busy schedules, they carved out time for their annual "Writer's Retreat." This self-proclaimed tradition involved escaping the city's clamor, renting a cozy cabin nestled amidst a serene mountain landscape. Here, amidst the whispering pines and the tranquil beauty of nature, they focused solely on their individual projects.

These retreats became their havens for creative rejuvenation. Long walks in the crisp mountain air sparked fresh ideas, and evenings spent by the crackling fireplace were filled with lively discussions about plot twists and character development. The solitude fueled their individual creativity, and the shared experience of their retreat strengthened the foundation of their friendship.

One particularly inspiring retreat, Ethan, struggling with a pivotal scene in his young adult fantasy novel, found himself captivated by a captivating legend Olivia shared about a hidden valley guarded by mythical creatures. The tale resonated with him, sparking a flurry of inspiration. He spent the next few days feverishly writing, fueled by Olivia's captivating narration and the breathtaking mountain scenery.

As the years progressed, their lives took unexpected turns. Olivia met someone special, a kind-hearted nature photographer who shared her passion for adventure. Ethan, ever the introvert, found himself cautiously dipping his toes into the world of dating, hesitant but hopeful.

Despite the changes in their personal lives, their friendship remained a constant. They celebrated each other's triumphs – Olivia's engagement, Ethan's first foray into public speaking – and offered unwavering support through life's inevitable challenges. Their bond, forged in the world of words, transcended romantic love, evolving into a deep and enduring friendship.

One crisp autumn evening, Ethan and Olivia sat on the porch of their familiar mountain cabin, a comfortable silence settling around them. Years had etched lines on their faces, but their eyes still sparkled with the same creative fire. As the first snowfall of the season painted the landscape in soft white hues, they reminisced about their journey – the shy online interactions, the awkward coffee shop meet-up, the exhilarating journey to literary success.

"Remember when we started this all those years ago?" Olivia mused, a nostalgic smile gracing her lips.

Ethan chuckled. "How could I forget? Nervous wrecks, both of us."

They shared a laugh, the warmth of their friendship radiating through the cool night air. Their story, once a tale of unrequited love and blossoming online friendship, had transformed into a beautiful testament to the power of shared passion, unwavering support, and the magic that unfolds when words weave a path to a lifelong bond. As they looked towards the star-studded sky, a silent promise hung between them – to keep writing, to keep exploring, and to forever cherish their extraordinary friendship, a story written not just in words, but in the enduring tapestry of their lives.

Chapter 5: Echoes of Inspiration

The scent of lavender and aged paper hung heavy in the air, a familiar comfort that enveloped Ethan as he stepped into Olivia's bookstore. Years had etched lines on their faces, a testament to the time that had flowed by since their mountain cabin retreats and the whirlwind success of "The Quirky Quills" series. Yet, their eyes still held the same spark of shared passion, a flicker that ignited whenever they were together.

Olivia, perched on a stepladder, reached for a book on the top shelf. Her movements were a tad slower, but her smile as bright as ever as she spotted Ethan. "There you are! I was beginning to think you'd gotten lost in the stacks."

Ethan chuckled, the sound echoing through the cozy bookstore. "Lost, maybe, but only in the sheer volume of stories. This place truly is a haven for bibliophiles." He ran his fingers along the spines of worn paperbacks, a nostalgic pang tugging at his heart. The bookstore, christened "The Inklings' Refuge," had been Olivia's dream, a haven for aspiring writers and a testament to their enduring love for the written word.

They settled into two plush armchairs tucked away in a quiet corner, a steaming mug of herbal tea warming Ethan's hands. They chatted about their latest ventures – Olivia's historical fiction novel nearing completion and Ethan's foray into screenwriting. Their conversation, infused with the ease of longtime friends, flowed effortlessly.

A comfortable silence descended as Ethan noticed Olivia gazing at a dusty typewriter tucked away in a display case. It was the very same typewriter she'd used to write her first novel, the one she'd confided in during their early online interactions. He remembered the vulnerability she'd shared in those messages, the raw emotions that had laid the foundation for their connection.

"Remember when you used to dream of publishing a book on that very machine?" Ethan asked gently.

A nostalgic smile touched Olivia's lips. "How could I forget? It feels like a lifetime ago."

Ethan's gaze lingered on the typewriter, a spark igniting within him. "Funny," he mused, "but I was just thinking about the mountain cabin. It wouldn't happen to be free this coming winter, would it?"

Olivia's eyes widened with a flicker of surprise, then a knowing smile spread across her face. "As a matter of fact, it is. What are you proposing, my friend?"

Ethan leaned forward, his voice filled with a hint of excitement, "What if we...? Well, what if we revisited the cabin one last time? Not just for a retreat, but for a new kind of collaboration."

A CRISP DECEMBER WIND whipped snowflakes around the familiar silhouette of the mountain cabin. Inside, however, a fire crackled merrily, casting a warm glow on Ethan and Olivia as they sat huddled around a worn wooden table. Years had passed since their annual retreats, but the cabin still held the magic of their early days – the haven where their stories began and where, perhaps, a new chapter was waiting to be written.

Ethan spread out a collection of weathered journals and loose scribbled notes on the table. "Alright," he began, a hint of nervous energy thrumming in his voice, "remember that idea I mentioned...?"

Olivia, her eyes mirroring his excitement, leaned forward. "The collaboration, yes? Tell me everything."

Ethan explained his proposition. They would write a new story together, not as the creators of the "Quirky Quills" series, but as a single entity under a new pseudonym. It was a bold idea, a return to their roots of anonymous online collaboration, fueled by the shared passion that had initially sparked their connection.

Olivia's brow furrowed in thought for a moment. "A new identity, huh? That brings back memories." A playful glint lit up her eyes. "But I like it. A chance to reinvent ourselves, to create something entirely new."

The following days were a whirlwind of brainstorming sessions fueled by steaming mugs of hot cocoa and the crackling fire. They delved into their well of experiences, weaving together fantastical elements with themes of enduring friendship and the transformative power of storytelling. The cabin, once more, became their sanctuary, a space where their creative energies collided and bloomed.

One evening, nestled in their respective reading nooks, they exchanged the first completed chapters. A nervous tension hung in the air as they delved into each other's work. A smile stretched across Olivia's face as she finished Ethan's chapter. "This is brilliant, Ethan! You've captured the protagonist's voice perfectly."

Ethan felt a wave of relief wash over him, replaced by a surge of pride as he read Olivia's chapter. "This is captivating, Olivia. The world-building is phenomenal!"

As the days turned into weeks, their collaboration flowed with an effortless rhythm. They critiqued each other's work with honesty and respect, their differences in style creating a rich tapestry of storytelling. They rediscovered the joy of their online collaboration, their shared passion for the written word a constant source of inspiration.

One particularly snowy afternoon, Ethan stumbled upon a hidden compartment in an old trunk tucked away in a dusty corner of the cabin. Inside, nestled amongst faded photographs and forgotten trinkets, lay a worn copy of "The Alchemist's Quest," the book that had sparked their very first debate all those years ago. He smiled, a wave of nostalgia washing over him.

That night, as they sat by the fire, Ethan recounted his discovery. Olivia's eyes widened with a flicker of amusement. "Remember our argument about the dragon's redemption?" she asked, a playful grin etching across her face.

Ethan chuckled. "How could I forget? Perhaps," he mused, gazing into the flames, "it's time to revisit that ending."

Olivia's smile widened, her eyes twinkling with excitement. "Now that's an idea I can get behind," she declared. "Let's give that dragon a second chance."

And as the fire crackled merrily in the hearth, casting long shadows on the cabin walls, Ethan and Olivia, their bond as strong as ever, embarked on a new chapter – a story not just written on paper, but woven into the fabric of their enduring friendship, a testament to the echoes of inspiration that resonated within the walls of their mountain cabin refuge.

Months flew by, punctuated by the satisfying clatter of keyboards and the buzz of creative energy that filled Ethan and Olivia's respective apartments. Their collaboration on the new novel, titled "The Dragon's Redemption," progressed with a renewed sense of purpose.

Gone were the pressures of deadlines and the expectations that came with their established names. This was a return to their roots, a pure exploration of storytelling, fueled by a shared passion that transcended fame or fortune. They emailed chapters back and forth, offering feedback and revisions, their online forum usernames – once a symbol of anonymity – now a cherished reminder of their journey.

One sunny afternoon, Ethan received an email notification. It was Olivia, her message accompanied by a new chapter titled "The Reckoning." He eagerly dove into the text, his heart pounding with anticipation. This chapter marked a pivotal point in their narrative, the moment where the protagonist, a young woman ostracized for her unconventional magic, was to face the fearsome dragon who terrorized her village.

As Ethan read, he was captivated by Olivia's masterful description. The tension crackled through the words, the fear of the villagers palpable. Yet, amidst the terror, there was a flicker of empathy, a hint of the dragon's pain and isolation. Ethan felt a surge of respect for Olivia's approach, a testament to her growth as a writer and her willingness to revisit their old debate.

When he finished the chapter, a smile stretched across his face. He knew exactly how to build upon it, to weave a path toward the redemption they'd both envisioned. He crafted his response, carefully constructing the dragon's inner turmoil, his desperate yearning for acceptance. He hit send, a thrill coursing through him as he awaited Olivia's reaction.

The following day, Olivia's response arrived, her email titled "A Bridge of Understanding." Her chapter explored the unexpected bond that formed between the young woman and the dragon, a connection forged through empathy and a shared sense of loneliness. Ethan devoured her words, his eyes welling up with emotion. Olivia's writing, always poignant, had reached a new level of depth and tenderness.

As they continued their collaboration, a sense of completion, not just of the story, but of their journey together, settled over them. They were no longer just online acquaintances or successful co-authors; they were storytellers who had grown alongside each other, their friendship a testament to the power of words and shared dreams.

One evening, as they video-called, the final draft of "The Dragon's Redemption" open on their respective screens, they shared a heartfelt laugh. "Remember how nervous we were about our first coffee shop meeting?" Ethan asked.

Olivia chuckled, a warm nostalgia radiating from her smile. "Who knew a chance encounter in an online forum would lead us here?"

They reminisced about their journey, the ups and downs, the triumphs and challenges. They had found not just literary success, but an enduring friendship that had enriched their lives in ways they could never have imagined.

"Ready to send it out into the world?" Olivia asked, her voice tinged with a hint of excitement.

Ethan, a grin splitting his face, nodded. "More than ready."

And with a click, they submitted the manuscript, their hearts filled with a quiet satisfaction. They knew that regardless of the outcome, the journey of creating "The Dragon's Redemption" had solidified their bond, a story not just for their readers, but a testament to the echoes of inspiration that resonated within their own hearts, a melody born in the online world and forever cherished in the warmth of their enduring friendship.

MONTHS MORPHED INTO a year, and news of "The Dragon's Redemption" reached a fever pitch. Published under their new, whimsical pseudonym, "The Inkwell Weavers," the book resonated with readers of all ages. The tale of the ostracized girl and the misunderstood dragon resonated with a profound message of acceptance and understanding. Critics lauded the novel's captivating narrative and the seamless blend of writing styles, praising the "Inkwell Weavers" for their unique storytelling voice.

One evening, Ethan and Olivia, nestled in their familiar armchairs at "The Inklings' Refuge," basked in the afterglow of their unexpected success. A stack of glowing reviews lay on the table, a testament to the positive reception of their collaboration.

"Who would've thought a return to our online forum roots would lead to this?" Olivia mused, a contented sigh escaping her lips.

Ethan chuckled. "And with a new twist – no more anonymous usernames. We're finally out in the open, a duo some reviewers are calling 'the masters of unexpected collaboration.'"

A comfortable silence settled between them, punctuated only by the soft clinking of teacups. Despite the newfound fame, their bond remained the same – a haven built on mutual respect, shared passion, and a deep appreciation for each other's talents.

Suddenly, a young woman with fiery red hair approached their corner, clutching a worn copy of "The Dragon's Redemption." Her eyes shone with admiration as she addressed them.

"Excuse me," she stammered, "are you the Inkwell Weavers?"

Ethan and Olivia exchanged a surprised glance.

"Yes, that's us," Olivia said warmly. "What can we do for you?"

The young woman, her voice trembling with excitement, explained how the story had resonated with her own struggles as an aspiring writer, feeling ostracized and misunderstood. "Thank you," she said, her voice thick with emotion, "for reminding us that even the most unexpected friendships can lead to something extraordinary."

Ethan and Olivia exchanged a heartfelt smile. This encounter, a testament to the impact of their story, filled them with a warmth that transcended awards and critical acclaim.

Later that evening, as they walked through the snow-dusted streets, the young woman's words echoed in their hearts. The journey that began with a chance online encounter had blossomed into a lifelong friendship and a successful literary partnership. They realized that the true magic wasn't just in the stories they created, but in the bond they had forged, a bond that resonated with a message of connection, a testament to the enduring power of words and the transformative beauty of friendship.

As they stood gazing at the city lights twinkling in the distance, a silent promise hung in the crisp night air. They would continue to write, to collaborate, to inspire, their journey a testament to the enduring echoes of inspiration that resonated within them, a melody that began in the online world and forever played on in the symphony of their extraordinary friendship.

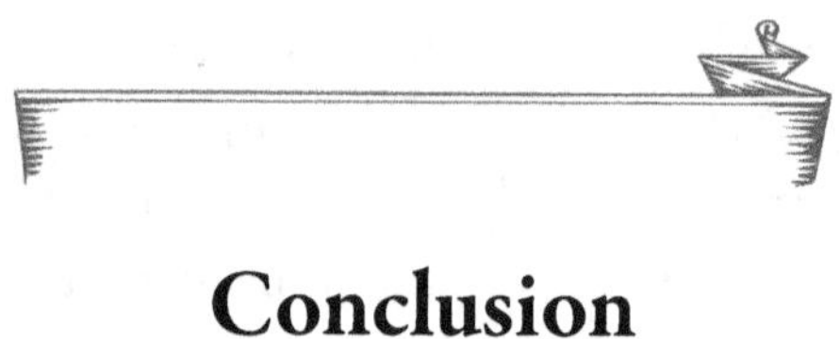

Conclusion

Ethan and Olivia, reunited by a chance encounter in their online forum, poured their hearts into crafting a new novel, "The Dragon's Redemption." Their collaboration, fueled by a shared passion for storytelling, transcended the boundaries of the digital world.

As they exchanged chapters and revisions, their online forum usernames – once mere aliases – became cherished emblems of their journey. Each chapter chipped away at the walls they'd built around themselves, fostering a newfound empathy and understanding.

With "The Dragon's Redemption" complete, they ventured out from their online haven, ready to share their creation with the world. The success that followed was a testament to the power of their collaboration, a melody born online that resonated with readers everywhere.

Yet, the greatest reward wasn't the acclaim; it was the enduring friendship they had forged. As they embarked on new chapters in their lives, they carried the echoes of inspiration within them, a reminder of the magic that bloomed from pixels to pages.

About the Author

Mrigendra Bharti, born on June 29, 2004, in South Delhi, India, is a multifaceted individual recognized as the owner of Mrigendra Bharti Group InfoTech India Co. Pvt Ltd. Beyond his entrepreneurial endeavors, he is a distinguished music producer, director, and a budding writer.

Embarking on his professional journey at a young age, Mrigendra Bharti's visionary leadership has led to the establishment of several successful ventures, including Croma Music Series Entertainment, Sellbrochure, Fauget Innovative, and more.

What sets Mrigendra apart is his early initiation into the world of business. His foray into the unknown realms of entrepreneurship began during his 10th-grade years, where he delved into the music industry. This initial venture laid the foundation for subsequent achievements, showcasing his dedication and resilience.

Having honed his skills in music, Mrigendra Bharti not only demonstrated significant growth in his craft but also expanded his professional network. His passion extends beyond music, encompassing app and website development, as well as graphic design.

Fueled by his creative aspirations, Mrigendra established the Mrigendra Bharti Group, a company specializing in website and app development. Currently, he collaborates with a dedicated team, collectively working on ambitious projects that promise innovation and excellence.

Mrigendra's journey serves as an inspiration, particularly for today's students, highlighting the potential of youthful determination and the ability to transform innovative ideas into successful businesses. As he continues to make strides in various domains, Mrigendra Bharti remains a dynamic force, contributing vibrancy to the realms of business, music, and technology.

Read more at https://www.imwriter-mrigendra.rf.gd.